I Can Read, Too

Puedo Leer, También

Book 5

Learn to Read Series

Cataloging-in-Publication Data

Sargent, Dave, 1941-
    I can read, too = Puedo leer, también. Book 5 /
by Dave and Pat Sargent ; illustrated by
Laura Robinson.—Prairie Grove, AR : Ozark
Publishing, c2004.
    24 p. : col. ill. ; 18 x 21 cm. (Learn to read series ; 5)

    Bilingual.
    Cover title.
    SUMMARY: Tells what a variety of animals can
do or like, such as a colt can run fast, a fox can be
sly, a mouse likes cheese, and a buffalo likes to roam.
    ISBN 1-56763-951-8 (hc)
          1-56763-952-6 (pbk)

    [1. Animals—Fiction.] I. Sargent, Pat, 1936-
II. Robinson, Laura, 1973- ill. III. Title. IV. Series.

PZ7.S2465Ic 2004
[E]—dc21   00-012635

Printed in the United States of America

I Can Read, Too
Puedo Leer, También
Book 5

Learn to Read Series

by Dave and Pat Sargent

Illustrated by Laura Robinson

Ozark Publishing, Inc.
P.O. Box 228
Prairie Grove, AR 72753

Dave and Pat Sargent, authors of the extremely popular Animal Pride Series, plus many other books, visit schools all over the United States, free of charge.

If you would like to have Dave and Pat visit your school, please ask your librarian to call 1-800-321-5671.

On the last page is a list of vocabulary words and the number of times each word is used.

bat-murciélago

colt-potro

sheep-oveja

lamb-cordero

fox-zorro

turtle-tortuga

pack rat-rata

mouse-ratón

buffalo-búfalo

I am a bat.
Yo soy un murciélago.

I live in a cave.
Yo vivo en una cueva.

I am a colt.

Yo soy un potro.

4

I can run fast.
Yo puedo correr rápido.

I am a sheep.
Yo soy una oveja.

I have wool.
Yo tengo lana.

I am a lamb.
Yo soy un cordero.

I am a little lamb.

Yo soy un cordero pequeño.

I am a fox.
Yo soy un zorro.

I can be sly.
Yo puedo ser astuto.

I am a turtle.
Yo soy una tortuga.

I can walk slow.
Yo puedo caminar despacio.

I am a pack rat.
Yo soy una rata.

I collect things.
Yo colecciono cosas.

I am a mouse.
Yo soy un ratón.

I like cheese.
Me gusta el queso.

I am a buffalo.

Yo soy un búfalo.

I like to roam.
Me gusta vagar.

Below is a list of 32 vocabulary words and the number of times each word is used.

a	11	in	1	to	1
am	10	lamb	2	turtle	1
bat	1	like	2	walk	1
be	1	little	1	wool	1
buffalo	1	live	1		
can	3	mouse	1		
cave	1	pack	1		
cheese	1	rat	1		
collect	1	roam	1		
colt	1	run	1		
fast	1	sheep	1		
fox	1	slow	1		
have	1	sly	1		
I	18	things	1		